A SHURIKEN COMET CHRISTMAS

JONATHAN EVAN HUDSON

Copyright © 2025 by Jonathan Evan Hudson

❀ Formatted with Vellum

A SHURIKEN COMET CHRISTMAS

BAH HUMBUG, *Humbug, Humbug, and Humbug—if you don't have enough Humbugs, we do.*

Of all the brilliant big glowing signs in Central Park of Fredericksburg, Virginia, there was no missing the big white glowing signage proclaiming that weird message in big blocky letters. Centered near the top of the red brick building of several windowless floors.

Even weirder—the only way in or out seemed to be a few upside-down L shaped pipes sticking out along the top ridge of the rooftop.

No hint of a door anywhere. Let alone any windows.

No way in or out—supposedly.

Yet rumor had it all the missing holiday whatevers that had been stolen a month ago in November—a bunch of gifts or somethings from kidlet charities in the area—those gifts were stashed inside that very building.

Why ... who knew? Not Jerome Higgins. It wasn't like those charities could afford Jermone and his rates.

Nope.

How that rumor even sprang into being—again,. Jerome Higgins didn't have the slightest clue.

He wasn't paid to dig up rumors. No. That was what super-lovely Asia bombshell Shea Ling and her amazing ninja skills were for. Including gathering intel on how to enter that very same Humbug-obsessed building.

Get the intel to Jerome within the next few minutes or else mission's off. No more pay either.

His ninja skills nowadays were more used to confirm—or discredit those rumors.

Often in a bloody violent and savagely secret way.

Bad enough the savory smell of some of the juiciest steak this side of anywhere and roasted potatoes seasoned just perfect with rosemary and parmesan came from the place next door. About several dozen feet to the right across a field of tall wild grass. Looking a diner of chrome glitz and colorful neon lights so bright sunglasses were needed to read any of the signage.

Never mind it was the ass crack of midnight.

Days from Christmas too, so Happy Holidays but not enough good cheer—yet. Least not until payday and hello presents for all the little kidlet cousins very, very soon.

So yeah.

Worth staying in this butt-freezing cold outside for the last few hours.

Finishing off the nice pricy less-than-healthy dinner of palm-sized tacos each filled with pale-red peppermint frozen custard. Tonight the custard didn't need any help staying solid and freshly cold. Nope. Even the messy gooey bits dropping here and there into the tall clusters of grass on along the ground.

Bits from the chocolate peppermint shell sealing the taco shut—until Jerome shattered some more of it open.

Other bits came from the decorations all over of red and green sprinkles. Sprinkles shaped like tiny bells and tinier mistletoe.

Some good red herring evidence to mislead whoever investigated this mess later.

Least according to the mysterious client who requested this exact red herring here and now.

Weirder and weirder but the guy paying the bills made the rules ... for the most part. He even called himself Mystery Minister, so yeah, weirdo all the freaking way to the moon and back, and tonight the moon was big enough for plenty of pale weird mystery.

From his left a spotlight suddenly lit the ground across from Jermone. Missing him by mere feet.

A beam of deathly white bright light. Only tall wild grass.

The beam wobbled ever so slightly. Whoever held the spotlight hurried in this direction.

But without a single crunch of grass erupting nearby?

Not in the plan. No guards were mentioned by Mystery Minister. Nothing "of consequence."

Let alone competent guards—

That instant.

From the corner of his sight. Jermone saw the second spotlight—from his right.

Turning toward him.

Fast.

He reacted just as instantly.

Somersaulting backwards. Over the beam of light. As it swept over the spot he had been standing only an instant ago.

Jermone landed silently. No grassy crunch. Nothing.

Now standing only a few feet behind where he had been standing a moment ago.

That ... these guards, or whoever they were, they were obviously more skilled than the usual rent-a-cop, or even the everyday hired goon.

Suddenly. Just then. The beam from the left. It swept toward him.

Jermone somersaulted again. Over the beam.

Landing just as silently.

The beams vanished. That instant. Silence.

His tacos gone too.

And soon Jermone too—to find Shea and get the hell out of there.

CHAPTER
TWO

SITTING on her knees Shea Ling once again pretended to seriously struggle against the steel cuffs binding her wrists tightly together behind her, then against the second steel cuffs binding her ankles tightly together, and the third steel cuffs binding the other two cuffs tightly together.

The pick to unlock all the cuffs was already in her fingers. Just like father trained her over and over again ever since she was a little girl.

But now wasn't the time to free herself.

Not yet.

Neither the pathetic canvas bag over her head nor the course cloth gag filling her mouth with long-dried peppermint coffee hid the sudden diminishing smell of fatty fragrant steaks and strangely seasoned potatoes from the nearby restaurant.

She was definitely inside the Humbug brick building—but none the wiser to how to get in.

Yet.

But soon she would—or fail badly.

Her shins and feet dug hard against slightly bending steel mesh. The mesh itself wobbled hazardously sideways, mostly, but also a little back and forth.

A low gruff grunt of some goon erupted behind her every so often.

But the constant mechanical squeal of cheap plastic wheels confirmed she was stuck currently in some kind of shopping cart. She must have broken enough goons during her pre-planned capture to earn this kind of treatment.

Jermone would be proud, probably, but also tease her about being on sale.

No aches let alone real injuries—yet.

The black leather of her ninja uniform protected her enough. For now. The goons didn't even take away any of her weapons—except her katana, her only obvious weapon.

None of her dozen of ninja throwing stars hidden throughout her uniform. None of her handful of kunai—even if these kunai were at best mere stylish throwing knives with thin light candy-cane-style handles and their fat short blades too wide and fat. Kunia she still hid in a few choice places as well.

Choice places serving as traps for the foolishly perverted and unwary—none of these goons, so far. Traps Jermone only pretended to be fooled by and Shea only humored Jermone and his playful physical teases too.

Teases Shea actually kinda hoped those teases would go further but—

Suddenly someone ripped off the canvas bag off her head. Flinging her long raven-black hair up around her face and especially her eyes.

Dosing herself with a weak whiff of the shea-scented shampoo and perfume their strange client, Mystery Minister, insisted Shea foolishly use tonight, despite the obvious foolish risk involved in doing so, in having any noticeable scent, pleasant or not.

But money was money and Shea needed money to cover her father's medical expenses.

Her hair fell aside an instant later.

And revealed the utterly unexpected.

Shea wasn't stuck in a shopping cart.

She was stuck in a mesh cage. A box cage barely bigger than herself sitting squarely on her knees. The cage itself was suspended a dozen feet above several raised rings of concrete doubling as seating for goth goons and their equally goonishly goth girlfriends.

The sudden jeer up from all of them all at once ... a powerful full-throated jeer.

Enough to flicker the dim lighting on-and-off quickly for a few moments. Just like those scary movies she was once obsessed with. The jeers even shuddered the steel mesh cage ever so slightly.

And the mechanical squeals weren't from wheels.

The squeals and squeaks came from four more cages. Each hung from a steel chain swaying off her cage. Each about half the size of her cage. And unlike hers those cages were fashioned out of ... bamboo?

Not steel.

And inside them ... shiny gift wrapped boxes of various sizes, colors, and shapes. Each with a even shinier bow tie and little folded card attached to the tie with a thing bright green string.

Presents? Christmas presents? Many of them,

But why?

These must be the stolen goods Mystery Minister wanted

her to find and for Jermone to recover so ... first to free herself from these cuffs with the pick quickly and—

A brutal roar erupted below Shea.

From some giant of a man—with a huge steel baseball bat in his right hand.

Dressed in colorful red and black spandex that showed off his ugly bulging muscles to the extreme. An even more colorful mask clung to his upper head. A mask of black, red, and green.

"Time for some Krampus Claus Chaos!" the man said.

Just as Shea picked herself free of the cuffs binding her wrists and ankles—but didn't shake them off just yet.

Now while the crowd jeered even louder. Focused too much on her. For now.

"Kill her! Kill her! Kill her!" the crowd cried.

"Is that all?" the spandexed man said. "That's just too pathetic. A simple quick death! When a long painful death will do much more nicely—and Krampus Claus just loves dealing out some serious pain, right folks!"

"Right!" the crowd said.

Before Shea could slip the pick back into her ninja uniform —BANG!

The cage suddenly jolted. From the baseball ball smashing into the side of her cage.

Denting her cage badly.

Worse—Shea dropped her pick. So escaping the cage— even more complicated now.

CHAPTER
THREE

JERMONE HUNG against the red brick wall like a spider clinging its own a gust-blown web, and wow, was it windy up here a couple dozen feet above the tall grass—quiet and still grass down there on the ground.

This Humbug building was taller than it even looked. Far taller. Kinda like Shea's crazy tough and over protective dad.

Not a hint of a window or door either. None.

If only this place wasn't as cold as Shea's mom was to him. Finger-freezing numb cold. Keep moving. Keep going. Don't stop or that freezing cold would truly become numbingly cold.

Despite his ninja gloves kinda sortof barely warming his hands.

Only way inside the building was, probably, on the rooftop. A few dozen feet above him. Maybe through, or into, one of those L-shaped pipes near the flat-looking rooftop's raised edge.

(Hopefully.)

If not for the pale milky moonlight climbing this wall would be near impossible—except the bricks were so regularly placed, the handholds so regular, good chance he could have done it with his eyes shut—except the beams of pale light kept swinging across the tall grass below.

Eventually they'd start swinging across the sides of this building too—but hopefully not too soon. Jermone had no other place to hide from all those beams.

Not until he reached the big block letters of glowingly bright white light.

Assuming there was a hiding place among those letters.

Big assumption—as big as Shea's tits he'd tease her—if she were here.

(Maybe earn a smack in the back of his head.)

((Maybe get a wicked sweet giggle too.))

First priority was finding Shea. Saving her if she needed saving. Big if.

As big as her tits kinda if.

It might be the goons that needed saving—not that he would save those louts.

A glance up at the middle two Humbug lights. In between them, between the "g" to the left and "H" to the right, on top of the comma in the middle, crouched ... squint, squint ... another ninja?

Yeah.

Least someone in a similar black leather ninja uniform. Similar lovely hourglass to heaven and back kinda figure as Shea, similar shape and size too, including that colossal chest ... but her figure ... it seemed a touch more petite than Shea's.

Then who ...

Jermone kept climbing. Just in case. Mystery Minister said nothing about backup.

Nothing about competent resistance either.

Shea never said anything about rivals either, let alone any sisters or friends or anything like that.

But Shea kept a lot of secrets from him. Like how her dad was sicker than he looked and the money for his medical expenses … wow. Insane. Jermone had his own secrets too. Plenty of them. She respected his so, of course, he'd respect her wishes to keep her secrets secret.

Until his life or worse, the mission required less discretion. Then—

A beam of light swept along the building. Passing a few feet above his hands.

Jermone didn't bother slowing down.

No.

He sped up. As fast as he could speed up.

No way to hide himself here. He was pretty much an easy target.

Until he reached those big block letters glowing brighter than any beam of light.

From his right another beam of light sped toward him. His legs would be revealed unless …

Just as it reached him Jermone hopped his feet up high. Hopping up the wall even higher.

Risking a horrible death-inducing fall but … what's life without a few risks?

The beam of light swept passed him. No one the wiser.

So far.

Until Jermone reached the giant blocky comma of the signage. No space to crawl between the comma and either the letter. Not the "g". Not the "H".

None.

A tsk from the ninja girl crouching on the comma.

"Shea partner as stupid as thought."

Her feminine voice had an arid sweetness to it. Unlike Shea.

Shea kept her voice as sweet as the honey she loved dumping into her morning green tea.

Jermone couldn't stop himself from wise-cracking back.

"Shea rival as ravishing as Shea—but ..."

The ninja girl somehow ducked down. Grabbed his wrist. Yanked him up hard and quickly. Helping him grab the ledge of the comma.

"Maybe boy not as dumb as told," the ninja girl said.

That this ninja girl smelled nicely of shea—just like that Mystery Minister insisted Shea smell like tonight—despite the obvious stupidity of it. This wasn't a date. Smelling at all was a danger. Pleasant or not.

"I'm Jermone, not boy."

"Cellow, not Shea."

Soon both his hands held the ledge of the comma. Held it tight. His feet propped against the low end of the comma. But his body ... block part of the blazing white light of the comma.

So, of course, cries came from below now.

Lost and lots of cries.

And then, no sign of the ninja girl Cellow now?

Until a moment later. Another arid sweet giggle. Still on top of the blocky comma but closer to the building's brick wall?

"Follow me inside, Jay-bird," Cellow said, "For a date to save Shea."

CHAPTER
FOUR

THE PROBLEM of Shea escaping the cage solved itself—when the cage exploded.

Literally.

One moment the small box of steel mesh shuddered—wobbling Shea more than slightly as she sat balanced on her knees. Mechanical squeals and squeaks erupted more and more around her. Mostly from the steel chains rattling and swaying off each corner of the cage's bottom.

More wooden creaks came from the bamboo cages hanging from the steel chains. Rattling and shaking the many gift-wrapped presents of various sizes and shapes within the bamboo cages.

At that same moment the crowd of goth goons roared their jeering approval.

A standing jeer.

The rings of concrete seats below—only one lone goth goon remained sitting. In back. Almost out of sight. Almost. Thanks to the people standing and jeering around the goon. That goon wore some weird but fancy red and black goth dress but the slim built of the goon—maybe a boyish girl, or a boy dressed as a girlish goth?

A goon maybe more important than the rest.

Maybe even more important than the muscled meathead below on the stage. The giant in thick spandexed black and red, and that upper head mask of green, red, and black.

The next instant the cage.

Gone.

Shattered.

Shattered like a glass smashed with a baseball bat.

A giant steel baseball ball. Swung powerfully hard.

The smell of broken steel. Of burnt steel. Thick in the air.

If Shea hadn't already freed herself she could have been in serious trouble as she fell straight down but no. She had already freed herself from the cuffs.

Swung the cuffs down. Spinning like a midair somersault.

Throwing all three cuffs quickly. In a row. Each like a slungshot.

Right at the giant.

At his beady-eyed head.

The giant. Rearing to smash Shea. Smash her like he had smashed the cage.

His giant steel bat. Barely dented. Only a little more scratched up.

Just as the giant started his deadly swing.

Shea threw a pair of ninja stars.

One star targeted the spot his wrist would soon be.

The other star—a spot along the middle of the bat. A spot where the bat would soon be.

His beady eyes jerked wide open—but the power of his movement—the terribly high speed—he was too committed to stop mid-movement.

Even to serve his arms, his bat out of the path of the stars.

A moment later his howl of agony.

Almost as loud as the crowd's sheer shrill jeer of fury.

And the moment, the distraction Shea needed to land safely on the giant's shoulders.

Then flipped backwards off the giant. Off his shoulder.

Forcing the giant to fall to his knees.

And Shea somersaulted onto the ground before the giant.

Just as the gifts around them. They all fell. Smashed into the concrete ground of the stage. Piles of presents. Scattered in piles around them.

But none shattered. None sounded broken? None looked broken?

Just as a metallic crack exploded above them. By the top of the steel chain that had held her cage up. Near the ceiling. Rattling the remains of the steel chain—but not dropping the chain. Not yet.

Worse.

The giant started laughing.

Laughing hard and furious.

"The bitch has spunk," the giant said.

Standing back up. Brushing off the star in his wrist. Brushing it off as if it was nothing.

"But," the giant said, "the real fun starts here!"

His spandex suit … it actually … actually protected him!

CHAPTER
FIVE

JERMONE LOVED a date with a pretty girl as much as the next guy but this tunnel seemed as dark and narrow as his chances of surviving this mess even if this Cellow ninja girl was on the up and up.

The floor. The ceiling. Even the walls.

All colder than the brick wall outside. Despite the stillness of the air. Freezing cold air. Cold enough that the heat of his own breath felt better than breathing the fresh freezing cold air.

No grips either. Just sheer sleek smoothness along the tunnel.

His ninja gloves weren't enough anymore. No where near enough to stay warm.

If Shea were here ahead of him he would have rubbed her leg with his freezing cold hand—still within the glove of course—to let her know of his situation without speaking out loud—even if it risked a teasingly vengeful kick back at him.

But Cellow wasn't Shea.

Better not say anything, yet. Sound echoed here,

throughout the whole tunnel. Speaking now risked the mission falling apart even worse.

But where were they headed?

The darkness was too dark to tell how far, or how close Cellow was to him—

His right hand landed on the back of a soft slim shin?

No flinch or jolt from Cellow either. Kudos to her for it too.

Not that Jermone could flinch his hand. Even had he wanted to.

Too numb with cold.

A familiar tsk erupted close ahead of him.

"Shea said you were touchy feelie but wow," Cellow said, "just hold on there—just not too tight. Your hand is colder than … nevermind. A few turns here and there and we'll be there."

"Good," Jermone said, "Any intel on that there?"

"On the way," Cellow said. "Don't you hear those jeers and roars up ahead? We're almost out of time. Shea can't hold them off for much longer—even if she thinks she can."

"Okay, okay," Jermone said, "you don't have to tell me twice. Let's hurry."

CHAPTER
SIX

SHEA DIDN'T KNOW how much longer she could hold out but surrendering was no longer an option—if it ever was one in the first place.

The flickering lights should have helped. Some. To hid her sudden movements—when timed just right. The noisy crowd hid any other noise other than that giant before her.

But for some strange unknown reason Shea felt a bit … dizzy. Unsteady on her feet. Very unlike her.

Especially during a mission.

The gift-wrapped presents scattered all around the round stage prevented her from darting around quick and silently. No hope of circling around the giant any time soon.

A single misstep and she'd trip or worse.

No time to recover—not with the speed that giant man could move.

The stage itself was tiny. Too tiny for a fight like this.

Barely a dozen feet wide and as round as Jermone's last overweight corgi. The giant took up more space than anything else here. As tall and wide with muscle as he was, the towering high walls of the concrete seating around them still dwarfed even him.

The walls loomed too high to even see the jeering crowd.

Only their roars of disapproval and bloodlust echoed loud and clearly down within the stage. No hope of seeing anyone else. Learning more about that strange goon who choose to remain seated, and seemingly silent.

The sheer sleek sides of the concrete stage—a difficult climb without potential interference from enemies.

Especially that giant.

The dark stains on the walls. Blood or worse. No effort to wash it away either. And the smells of dried blood. Of dried sweat and worse.

Good chance people died here and were never heard of again.

And so would she if she fell here.

If only she could fell the steel chain above her at the right moment—drop the steel chain onto the giant and his head but her first attempt failed badly. Revealing her scheme. Preparing the giant for another try—if she was so foolish to try again, and too obviously.

But no. She needed a different plan. Another way out of this mess.

None of her ninja stars. None of her kunai. None of them were sharp enough to pierce that suit of his. Aiming for spots not covered—too obvious too. Like his eyes. His lower face.

The giant crouched some, and barked another laugh, and smirked sinister.

"Frightened now, little girl?" the giant said. "Don't know what to do? Then die!"

Shea hopped backwards.

Just in time. Dodging the first swipe of his massive left hand.

But the second swipe. Of his right massive hand.

It brushed her.

Yet it sent her flying sideways. Feet barely able to reach the ground. Slow her down. The stale air gushing around her. Her legs smashing into presents.

Bang. Bang. Bang.

Then. Last moment. Her feet. Touching the ground.

Stumbling. Stumbling too fast to even slow down.

Until crash!

Into the concrete wall. A crash so powerful Shea bounced off the wall. Fell to her knees. Fell before she could stop herself. Could catch her balance.

A gasp. A rasp.

Her breath.

Shea could barely breath now.

And the giant. He loomed before her.

Both hands stretched out wide. Readying to clap her. Readying all his might to crush her.

Ready to end the match in the most obvious way possible.

And Shea. If only.

If only she had said something to Jermone sooner.

Father knew how she felt. Mother too. They'd miss her as much as Shea would miss them.

Shea tried to say something. Anything to delay the inevitable.

But only a mumbled moan came out.

A moan that got the giant laughing in even more sadistic glee.

"Cat got our tongue?" the giant said. "No! The wolf ate your tongue! And the rest of you coming up!"

If she somehow survived this ...

Jermone ... despite all the many troubles they've both gone through these last few years ... she never admitted they seemed more than mere partners in crime and ... despite his teases getting more and more physically ... intimate, so ...

A tingle down her spine. Despite the crowd roaring in bloodthirsty approval.

Shea didn't dare looked for the backup she sensed was nearly here.

In fact ... better distraction the enemy from incoming help.

So Shea gasped, more like rasped.

"Do your worse ..." Shea said. "you big buffoon."

And she slumped down—feinting more exhausted injury than she really felt.

JERMONE STOOD on all fours in shock. Mostly in shock.

The wobbliness of the steel beam he was crawling on ensured he didn't ever get too shocked still—or else he'd fall down and doom them all.

The steel beam itself was barely wide enough to support Jermone. Several feet ahead of him Cellow crawled along the same steel beam. Her petiteness let her fit slightly better on the beam but not by much.

Jermone had to counter wobble her wobbles or else no telling whether they'd fall together or the beam would fall with them.

Several dozen feet down was what Jermone came for—and unfortunately for Shea she was doing his part of the job and fairing poorly—just like how he faired laughably poorly last time he tried doing her role when she was too sick to do so.

That round pit of concrete. Concrete stained with plenty of dried blood and worse.

Shea was near the opposite side.

A huge hulk of a man in shiny latex catsuit. Weirdly

colored red, black, and the mask had some green to it too. That howling freak of a hulk already had his freakishly large hands stretched wide out.

As if about to make a loud powerful clap.

Shea in the center of that clap.

Around the pit. Above it. Rings and rings of goth guys and girls. The kind carrying actual weapons of the sharp and illegal kind, and not just part of their ugly black and steel-studded outfits.

Except for one lady ... guy ... whatever in a red and black dress of ... another weirdo since that goth guy ... or girl only scowled at everyone. No cheering or jeering.

Just annoyed impatience.

The lights flickered too much in sync with the cheers and jeers of the crowd. Why Shea wasn't able to use those flickers .., as obvious as the timing was ... least it was butt-freezing cold in here. Al the people and their evil roars. That warmed the place up plenty.

But nothing compared to a nice cuddle with a girl like Shea —and once he saved her again maybe he'd ... no. Let her recover from this mess without any awkwardness this time.

Which meant he'd need to save Shea and quickly.

No hope of jumping down and doing any good—he'd only break his legs at best.

Sure he had ninja stars and kunai similar to Shea hidden throughout his ninja uniform but that latex might be protective but fake shiny leather instead. Protective enough against any stars and kunai he could throw up here.

But that thick damaged steel chain hanging above the hulk ... a steel chain closer and closer to him as he crawled toward it, as he crawled along the beam.

Perfect.

Cellow had already reached the other side of the beam. Motioned him to follow her into another dark and narrow tunnel. As if Shea would survive long enough if he didn't do something right now.

So Jermone grimaced at Cellow. Shook his head.

And waved her to go on without him.

Since at that moment Jermone reached the steel chain. Grabbed it.

It squeaked with strain—but didn't break.

Until he leapt onto it.

Then snap!

CHAPTER
EIGHT

SHEA HEARD the metallic snap above her. A snap she refused to react too. Her strange dizziness helping her act defeated and ready to die. Her back near the concrete wall. A wall full of plenty of blood stains and worse.

The roar of the crowd must have hid the metallic snap from the giant.

The flicker of the lights. Their timing. They sealed the giant's fate.

Even as the giant tensed his bulging muscles. About to clap his hands into Shea from both sides. Smash her. Crush her. Probably several times to finish her all.

But too late—for the giant.

No missing Jermone hollering right above him.

"One air drop!" Jermone said, "For the fugly freak below!"

The giant released a "huh?"

Just as the steel chain smashed landing onto the giant's head. Knocking the giant downward.

Jermone landed feet first onto the giant's thick shoulders. Slamming the giant down.

Down flat into the concrete ground.

Standing victoriously on the giant Jermone smirked with his eyes down at Shea.

"Ninjas a nice perfect three," Jermone said, "and Humbug Losers, a big fat zero—"

Despite the howling of boos and worse. Shea reacted before she knew why. Sensed the the real attack an instant before it was too late.

Shea flung several ninja stars up above her.

Clank!

Clank!

Clank!

Smacking aside several ninja stars that had been thrown at Jermone. Thrown by ...

Standing on a steel beam above and behind Shea ... a ninja girl that looked far too much like Shea herself when in a ninja uniform ... it couldn't be ... but—

"Enough showboating, you two!" Cellow said.

Shea stumbled backwards. Dizzy again for some unknown reason. Probably one of those mild poisons her twin sister Cellow was all too notorious for. That Cellow choose to come and interfere here and now ... after years ignoring Shea and ...

Someone caught her. Someone with a familiar steady grip and—

"Jermone," Shea said, "I ... I ..."

Shea gulped. No doubt what kind of teasing Cellow inflicted on Jermone.

"Good timing," Shea said, "for a ninja date."

Jermone held, then hugged her firmly, from behind. His uniform ... so cold? It ...

"Good," Jermone said, "I need some heating and you're perfect for the job."

"You know what else is perfect?" Shea said.

Before Jermone could ruin the moment with his incoming quip Shea dropped a smoke bomb.

Just as someone shouted: "Police! The police found us! Run!"

And soon it wasn't just Jermone and Shea on the run.

CHAPTER
NINE

ESCAPING a concrete pit quickly and silently enough proved more than what Jermone and Shea could manage, especially together, and Jermone wasn't about to abandon Shea.

Not here.

Not ever.

The smoke from the bomb Shea dropped darkened everything around them. Made breathing a bitch worse than his last corgi nagging him for her seventh meal of the day. Least the smoke was almost as warm as Shea leaning against him.

Her slim soft body warmed him in far more ways than one.

Enough that he might manage an escape—if a distraction at the right moment came their way.

Maybe.

If they had any luck left.

But by the time the smoke cleared from Shea's bomb it was obvious that no, they wouldn't escape this time.

Serious legal nonsense incoming instead.

Around the concrete ring police already stood. All looking

down. Pistols drawn out and aimed down. Ready to rain death upon both Jermone and Shea if either gave them the slightest excuse to fire.

The lights didn't even had the decency to flicker again.

Even as that weird guy, or girl, in that red and black dress strolled up to the edge of the pit. In his hand was a police badge?

"Let me guess," Jermone said, "Mystery Minister. Here to end the day."

The guy tsked. Scorn all over his face.

"Just surrender," he said, "and maybe you'll get a decent deal this time. Thanks to you we got all the goons and recovered all the gifts ... even if some are broken ... better some saved then none at all."

"No holiday forgiveness?" Jermone said. "Where's your holiday spirit?"

"We're the police," the guy said, "not Santa—"

The lights flickered right at the instant. Off then on. Off then on.

Till crack!

The sound of lights shattering.

"Shit!" the guy said. "The third ninja's still up there!"

Just as Jermone felt a rope slap his hands. A hanging rope that withstood a solid tug.

A solid escape plan now.

CHAPTER
TEN

SLIDING out of a cold steel pipe and rolling onto the flat rough rooftop of the brick Humbug building Shea climbed to her feet. The freezing cold air jabbing away the last of the dizziness that had plagued her earlier. Poison no doubt to ensure the police didn't take the enfeebled Shea too seriously.

Until it was too late.

Around the Humbug building sirens flashed and screamed. Police cars were being loaded with goth goon prisoners but no ninjas, thanks to Cellow and her last moment light shattering escape scheme.

But that didn't excuse Cellow from joining in and cuddling with Jermone as much as Shea was, all on the excuse that Jermone needed the warmth, and Shea couldn't provide enough by herself.

Nor didn't it excuse Cellow from her girlish giggles every time Jermone wiggled around, as if the rough ground of the rooftop bothered him, or that he wasn't obviously enjoying the silly scents that awful Mystery Minister had convinced both

Shea and Cellow to wear on a mission, as if it was a date rather than a mission.

Obviously it was meant to track them but up here none of those police dogs could hope to find them. No matter the scent.

Least for now.

There wasn't any other way to reach this rooftop except through those pipes anyway.

So cuddling Jermone in what he jokingly said was a lovely sandwich—Shea simply looked up at the twinkling stars. the huge bright moon, and ... a few falling stars?

Cellow giggled. "We'll need a name for our team ..."

"A name ..." Jermone said. "I think I know one ..."

Shea pinched Jermone quiet. "A good one. Not a joke. Like Shuriken Comet."

Jermone sighed, clearly disappointed.

Until Cellow giggled again.

"Shuriken Comet sounds great," Cellow said. "So—"

Jermone gave Shea and Cellow an overly familiar hug that ... he should have only shared with Shea but ... sigh.

"To a Shuriken Comet Christmas then," he said.

"And for a better payday next year!" Shea and Cellow said together.

And this time they all giggled together.

WANT MORE?

Go to
www.JonathanEvanHudson.com